SIMON AND SCHUSTER

SIMON AND SCHUSTER
First published in Great Britain in 2013 by Simon and Schuster UK Ltd
1st Floor, 222 Gray's Inn Road, London WC1X 8HB
A CBS Company

Based on the television series Mike the Knight
© 2013 HIT (MTK) Limited/Nelvana Limited. A United Kingdom-Canada Co-production.

ISBN 978-1-4711-1595-0
Printed and bound in China
10 9 8 7 6 5 4 3 2 1
www.simonandschuster.co.uk

Mike the Knight and the Wizard's Treasure

Mike is searching
high and low.
His dragon friends
are in the know.
They've set our knight
a clever test,
and now he's on a
treasure-hunting quest!

Great knights search for hidden treasure—even if the trail is dark and dangerous!

One morning the dragons set Mike his own special treasure hunt. They placed arrows throughout the castle.

"Getting warm," said Squirt, as Mike followed their arrows to Evie's workshop.

Mike lifted Evie's hat off the floor and found an apple underneath.
"It's a golden colour," said Mike, "just like **REAL** treasure."

"My book says that there's treasure hidden in
the Maze Caves!" said Evie.
"Real treasure?" gasped Mike.
Evie nodded. This wasn't just real treasure,
it was **WIZARD'S** treasure.

"By the King's crown, that's it! I'm Mike the Knight and my mission is to go to the Maze Caves and find the wizard's treasure!"

Mike scrambled up to his bedroom and pulled the secret lever on the wall. He drew his enchanted sword. "A roll of ribbon?" he groaned. "How will that help me find the treasure?"

"Don't worry," said Squirt. "You'll find the treasure in no time…"
"…unless it's guarded by Cave Monsters!" chipped in Sparkie. Cave Monsters weren't going to stop this brave knight.

"There are clues in my book," announced Evie, "pictures of wizards' hats!"

Mike frowned. Everyone knew that treasure-hunting was a knight's job, not a wizard's. He galloped off to the Maze Caves, leaving Evie behind.

As soon as they got to the Maze Caves, Mike jumped
off Galahad and ran inside. "This way," he called. "Let's
find the treasure!"

Squirt felt nervous. He hoped there weren't any Cave
Monsters around!

Mike pointed to a wizard's hat carved into the rock. "It's a clue!" he decided.

Squirt gulped. This was just the kind of place where a Cave Monster would live.

Luckily Mike had an idea.

"Do a really loud roar. That will scare any Cave Monsters away!"

GGgggrrr!

"We'll see who's best at finding treasure," Evie muttered as she followed Mike into the Maze Caves...

"GGggggrrr!"

"A Cave Monster!" Quick as a flash, Evie pulled out her wand.

"Wizard's magic, fizz and crack! Make those Cave Monsters stay back!"

Evie's wand sent a blast of stars and smoke swirling through the caves.
"What's that?" spluttered Sparkie.
"It's magic," frowned Mike. "Evie must be hunting for treasure too!"

Mike had to find the treasure before Evie did!

Mike spotted another wizard's hat.

"It's a clue," he grinned. "Come on, dragons!"

Squirt thought that the path to the treasure looked a bit spooky. He did lots of roaring to keep the Cave Monsters away.

When Evie heard more roaring, she decided to cast a soapy spell.

"Now the Cave Monsters are attacking us with bubbles!" shrieked Squirt.

"It's just Evie again," sighed Mike.

Mike and his friends made their way through the Maze Cave tunnels and found another wizard's hat on a door.

"We've found the treasure!" said Mike.

Squirt let out an extra-fierce roar. Treasure meant Cave Monsters!

GGggggrrr!

Evie pulled out
her wand.

*"Wizard's magic,
one more time.
Keep those Cave
Monsters in line!"*

Tickle-Tangler
vines appeared!
Mike and the
dragons were
trapped!

Mike let out a loud laugh – the magic vines were tickling him! His giggles were so loud, even Evie could hear them.

"Oh no! The Cave Monsters must have got Mike!" The worried wizard-in-training ran towards the noise as fast as she could.

Mike heard Evie calling for him.

"The Cave Monsters must have got Evie," he shouted. **"It's time to be a knight and do it right!"**

Mike struggled free and drew his sword. "We'll use the ribbon to find our way back."

Mike ran and ran... straight into Evie!
"I thought the Cave Monsters had got you!" they both
said at the same time.
"GGggggrrr!" said Squirt. "I've come to scare
the Cave Monsters!"
Evie rubbed her eyes. The scary noise had been Squirt
all along!

"I'm sorry, Evie," said Mike. "Let's get the treasure **TOGETHER.**"

The pair followed the ribbon all the way back to the door at the end of the tunnel.

"Look!" gushed Evie. "There's a gap in the stone."

The gap was the same shape as Evie's wand.

Evie pressed her wand into the gap.

The stone door suddenly slid away. There was a large wooden chest inside the chamber.

"Wow!" gasped Mike.
"The treasure's in that box," said Evie. "Let's open it together."

A purple wand floated out of the treasure chest.

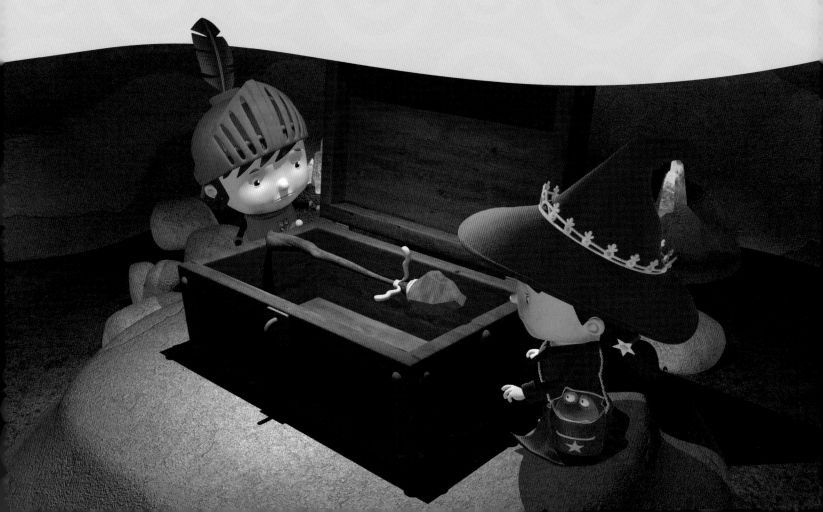

"I've read about these," beamed Evic, leaping onto the wand. She whizzed around the chamber, laughing all the way.

Mike chuckled. A flying wand was the perfect kind of treasure for a wizard!

"HUZZAH!"